A Coat of Cats

Jeri Kroll
&
Ann James

CANCELLED

Lothian
BOOKS

For Moonlight, Alethea and Shadow,
and in memory of Tenzing and Hillary

JK

For old friends: Tux, Jack, Min and Mac, Victor, Moshe,
Fungus, Ella and the ginger cat;
and new friends: Betsie, Bobbie, Bruce and Bart and Bruce

AJ

Thomas C. Lothian Pty Ltd
11 Munro Street, Port Melbourne, Victoria 3207

Text copyright © Jeri Kroll 1998
Illustrations copyright © Ann James 1998

National Library of Australia
Cataloguing-in-Publication data:

Kroll, Jeri, 1946–.
A coat of cats.
ISBN 0 85091 953 3.
I. James, Ann. II. Title.
A823.3

Designed by Lynn Twelftree
Illustration medium: chalky pastel on coloured paper
Printed in Hong Kong by Wing King Tong

Once there was an old woman
who lived alone.
Or so her neighbours said.

But she didn't live alone.
She lived with
seven cats.

'A lot of cats,' said the neighbour on the left.
'Too many cats,' said the neighbour on the right.

Just enough, the old woman thought.
She had cats of every kind (she could find)
and they were her family.

One cat slept at the foot of her bed.

Two cats slept perched on her chair.

One cat slept wrapped around her head.

A couple curled in a bottom drawer

The old woman and the cats walked
in her little square of garden.
The cats wore bells around their necks
to warn the birds.

When they leapt together onto the backyard
fence, they tinkled like wind chimes.

On cool nights they purred by the fire.
The old woman purred loudest of all.

One winter's day, a man from the Town Hall
came to tell the old woman she had to move.
'Your house is old and dangerous,' the man explained.
The woman was old, but she didn't feel dangerous.

'You can move to a nice new flat
on the other side of town.'

The old woman didn't know the other side of town.
She liked it just where she was, and told the man so.

'You'll love the shiny new flat,' he said.
'But you'll have to leave all those cats.'

The old woman said she'd stay then,
thank you very much, and closed the door.

But they moved her anyway.

They put her clothes in big brown boxes.
They put her bed and armchair in a truck
and drove to the other side of town.

The cats stayed.

When some people came to try to catch them,
the cats slipped away like whispers on the breeze.

Then they drifted back, one by one.

They prowled around the boarded-up house.

They yowled like seven babies with wet nappies.

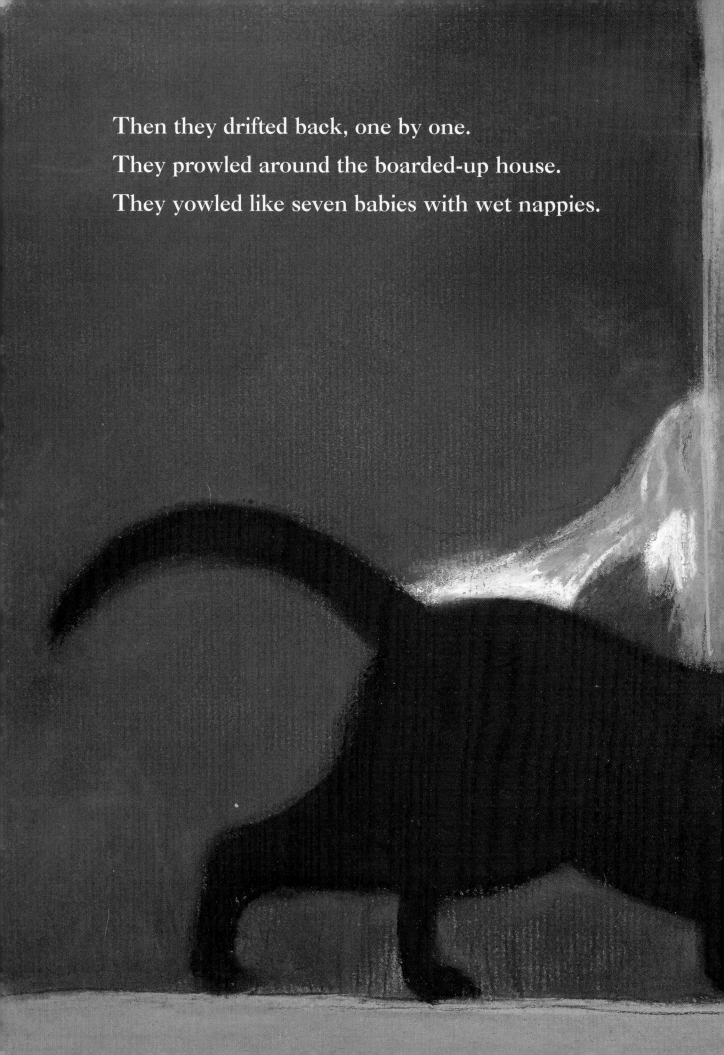

One night, the old woman dreamed
she heard them calling.
She woke up and thought,
Maybe they're hungry, or thirsty, or lonely.

So she went to see.

It was very far and very cold.
She took leftovers and a thermos of tea.

The cats saw her coming.

She fed them all the scraps,
then sat down on the doorstep and fell asleep.

Frost coated her eyelids.
Icicles outlined her nose.
Her tea froze.

The cats circled around.

They settled in heaps in her lap.

They washed her face and scoured her hands.

They curled up in the crooks of her arms.

They wrapped themselves over her legs.

They petted and pampered,

they rubbed and wriggled

into a coat of cats to keep her warm.

And they began to hum.

They crooned themselves into her dreams.

They melted the icicles into streams.

They harmonised jazzy summer tunes.
They sang so hot they sang down the moon.
They sang so sweet the old woman purred.

They sang so loud the old woman stirred

and s t r e t c h e d . . .

and smiled at the morning sun.

A new day had begun . . .

for everyone.